Pictures
by
Leonard
Weisgard

Story
by
Margaret
Wise
Brown

Copyright renewed 1970 by Leonard Weisgard. —ISBN 0-06-020821-X (lib. bdg.)
ISBN 0-06-020820-1.
ISBN 0-06-443003-0 (pbk.)
Library of Congress Catalog Card Number 92-46879
New Edition, 1994.

THE INDOOR NOISY BOOK

HarperCollinsPublishers

The little dog Muffin had a cold.

You can't go outdoors Muffin, they said. You

have to stay in the house all day and sleep

a lot in your own little bed.

So what could Muffin do?

He curled up in his bed

and closed his eyes

and cocked his ears

and there he was.

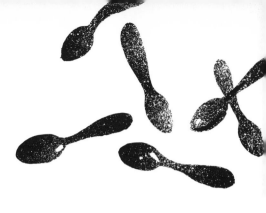

All about him he could hear the noises in the house.

He could hear a broom sweeping

swish swish swish

Somebody taking the spoons off the table

clank clank clink clank

A telephone

ding a ling ring

A vacuum cleaner

mmmzzzmmmmmmmm

And the cook in the kitchen beating eggs

bbbbbbbbbbbbbbbb

He could hear someone turning on the bath

swishshshhhsssss

Then Muffin heard someone dropping a pin.

Or could he hear that?

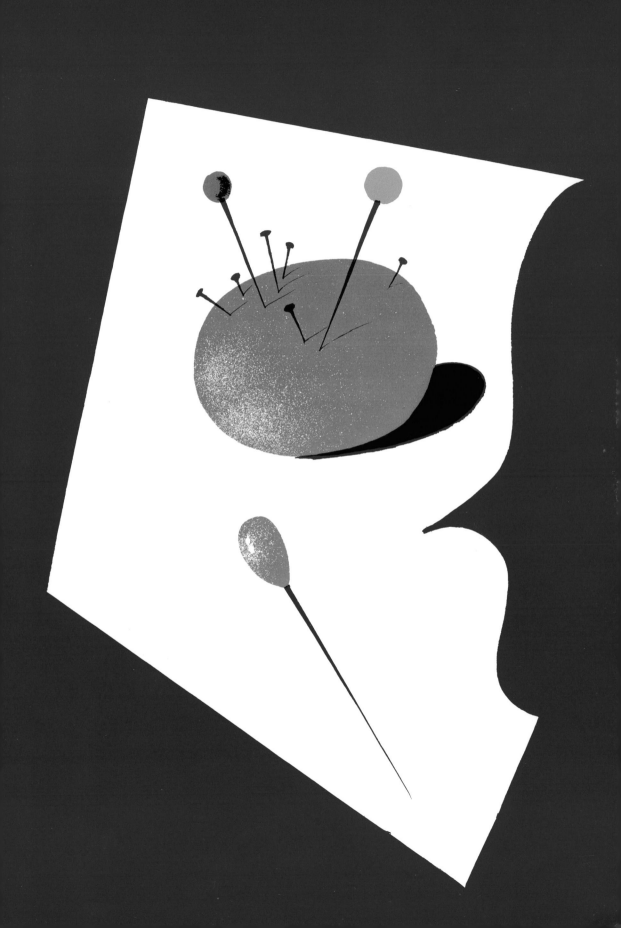

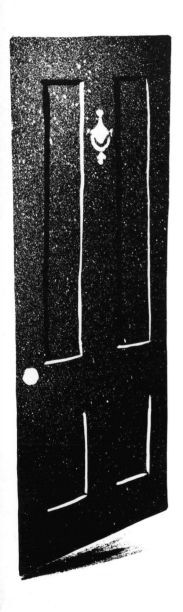

And he heard a fly buzzing
    How was that?
And he heard a wasp
    How was that!
And someone slammed the front door
    How was that?
Someone else was reading a book
    But could Muffin hear that?

And then there was a rattle of dishes. That
meant lunch.

> What kind of noise did lunch make?

They had celery for lunch

> Could Muffin hear that?

And soup

> Could Muffin hear that?

And raw carrots

> and steak

>> and spinach

> Could Muffin hear that?

And some very quiet custard for dessert

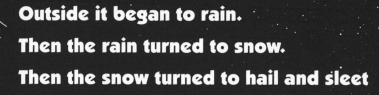

Outside it began to rain.

Then the rain turned to snow.

Then the snow turned to hail and sleet

hssssssss ping ping ping

Everything got white outside.

In the room everything got gray.

Muffin could hear the wind

whoo whoo whoo

And the sleet and snow

And the cars on the snowy road

How was that?

It began to get dark.

And all over the town the lights turned on
all at once.
    But could Muffin hear that?

NO

But Muffin did hear them turn on the light
in his own room

      click

And then all around him was warm electric
light.

And he could hear everyone coming up the
stairs to see the little dog who had a cold.

First he could hear the little boy's feet
coming up the stairs

      How was that?

   pat pat pat pat

Then he could hear the little boy's mother's footsteps

How was that?

patter patter patter

Then the little boy's father's footsteps

How was that?

clump clump clump

Then the cook's footsteps

How was that?

Dump Dump-de-dumma-de Dump

Then he heard some little tiny footsteps
coming to see him.

Muffin could just hear them coming softly
up the stairs.

Was it a little bug coming to see Muffin?

NO

Was it an elephant coming to see Muffin?

NO

Was it a soldier?

NO

Was it a sailor?

NO

Was it a duck?

NO

Was it a clown with a firecracker?

NO

Was it a whiskered mouse?

NO

What could it be?

It was the cat, of course.

And the cat came right into the room.

Everyone brought Muffin a present.

And the cook brought him his dinner and

they all watched him eat it.

The next day Muffin didn't have a cold any

more and he went outdoors again and listened

to the birds and the trucks.